Big Bear to the Rescue

By Richard J. Margolis
Pictures by Robert Lopshire

GREENWILLOW
A Division of William Morrow &
New York

 Inquiries should be addressed to Greenwillow Books, William Morrow & Company, Inc., 105 Madison Ave., New York, N.Y. 10016.
Printed in the United States of America.

1 2 3 4 5 79 78 77 76 75

Library of Congress Cataloging in Publication Data

Margolis, Richard J Big Bear to the rescue.
(Read-alone series)
SUMMARY: A cumulative series of trades results when Big Bear tries to borrow a rope to rescue Mr. Mole.
[1. Friendship—Fiction] I. Lopshire, Robert.
II. Title. PZ7.M3357Bi3 [E] 75-8583
ISBN 0-688-80005-X ISBN 0-688-84005-1 lib. bdg.

for all rushers to the rescue

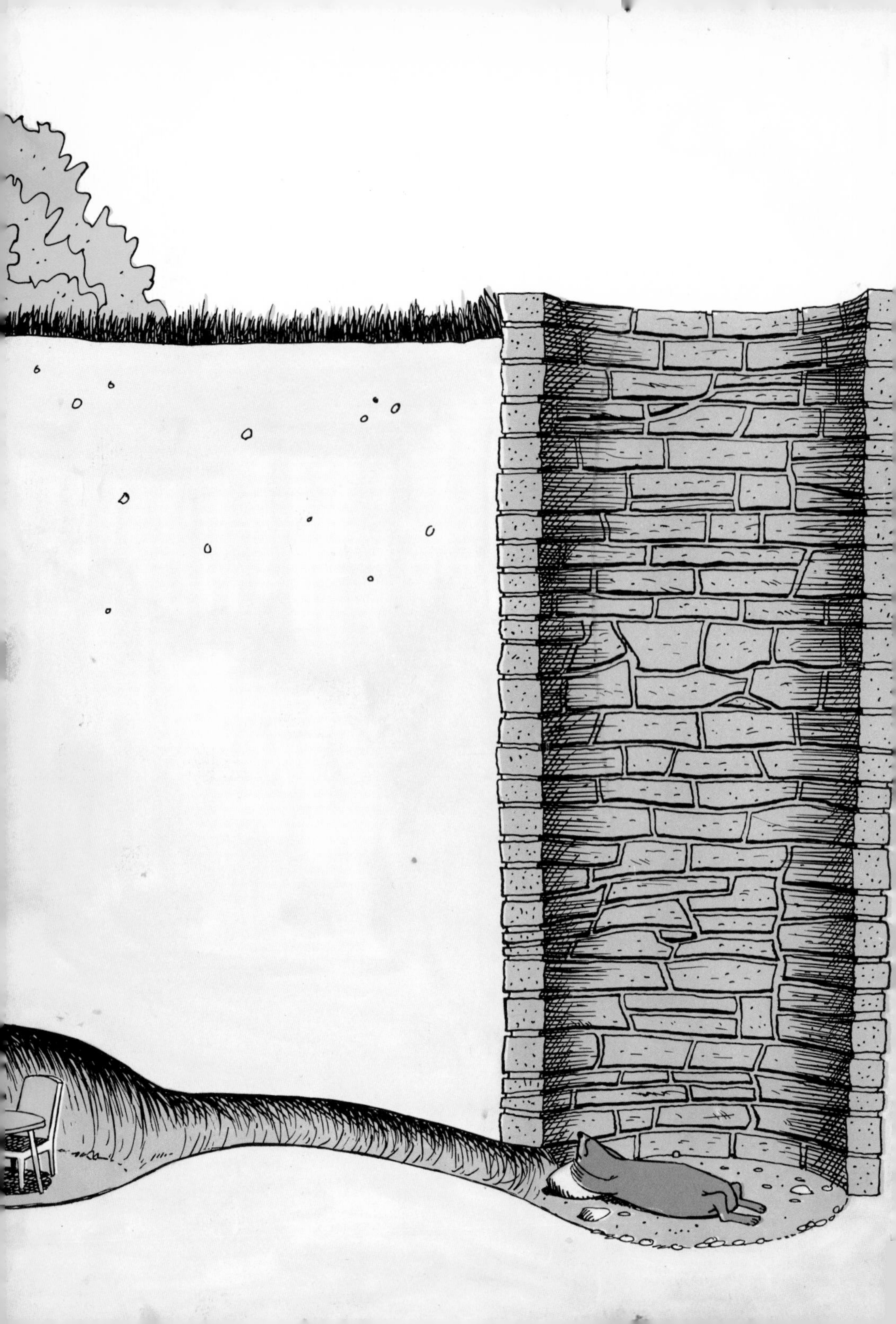

Mr. Mole lived in a secret tunnel.
The tunnel started with a hole
in Skunk's yard.
It ended at the bottom
of an old well.
Nobody used the well
because it was dry.
But Mr. Mole
liked to take naps there.

One day Big Bear
walked by the well.
He looked down and saw
Mr. Mole sleeping in the well.

"Oh, my goodness," said Big Bear.
"Poor Mr. Mole
has fallen in the well."
Big Bear lay down and
stuck his head into the hole.
"Mr. Mole," he called.
"Mr. Mo-o-ole."
Mr. Mole didn't stir.
"Oh, dear," cried Big Bear.
"He's been knocked out!
I must rescue him."
And he ran off to look for a rope.

Soon he met Squirrel.
Squirrel was sitting by the road
looking at a pile of bricks.
"Quick, Squirrel," said Big Bear.
"I need a rope to rescue Mr. Mole,
who has fallen in the well."

Squirrel did not look up.
"That's terrible," he said.
"I'd like to help.
But first I must carry
these bricks to my house.
If you can find me a wheelbarrow,
Big Bear, I'll give you a rope."
"Thank you, Squirrel,"
said Big Bear. And he ran off.

Down the road he saw Owl.
"Quick, Owl," called Big Bear.
"I need a wheelbarrow for Squirrel,
so he can get me a rope
to rescue Mr. Mole,
who has fallen in the well."

Owl blinked.

"Count on me, Big Bear.

I think I know

where I can find a wheelbarrow.

But right now

I have to feather my nest.

If you can find me a soft pillow,

I'll get you a wheelbarrow."

"That's very nice of you,"

said Big Bear. And he ran off.

Soon he saw Spotted Pony
eating grass by the road.
Big Bear was breathing hard.
"Quick, Spotted Pony," he shouted.
"I have to find a pillow for Owl,
so he can find a wheelbarrow
for Squirrel,
so he can get a rope
to rescue Mr. Mole,
who has fallen in the well."

Spotted Pony was trying
to scratch his back.
"That's a very sad story,"
he said.
"I'll look for a pillow.
But first I have to get
these flies out of my mane.
Find me a brush,
and I'll find you a pillow."
"Thank you, Spotted Pony,"
said Big Bear.

Big Bear ran to Skunk's yard
at the end of the road.
Skunk was eating a piece of toast.
Big Bear collapsed on the grass.
"Quick, Skunk," he gasped.
"Mr. Mole has fallen in the well,
and I need a brush to rescue him."
"What?" said Skunk.
"How are you going to rescue
Mr. Mole with a brush?"
Big Bear sighed.
"It's a long story.
Just give me the brush, Skunk."

Skunk took a tiny bite of toast.
"Sure," he said.
"As soon as I've finished eating
this very dry piece of toast."
Then he added, "Of course,
I'd get done a lot faster
if I had some honey."

Big Bear jumped up.
"Honey?" he said.
"I have lots of honey at home."
Big Bear ran to his house.
He got a jar of honey
and took it to Skunk.
Skunk gave him a brush.

Then Big Bear raced
across the field to Spotted Pony.
“Now hurry and get the pillow,”
said Big Bear, putting the brush
in Spotted Pony’s teeth.
“And meet me in Skunk’s yard.”

Big Bear ran up the road.
He passed Owl.
"You'll find a soft pillow
in Skunk's yard," he shouted.
"And don't forget the wheelbarrow."

Finally, he came to Squirrel.
Squirrel hadn't moved.
"Okay, Squirrel," said Big Bear.
"There is no time to lose.
Bring the rope to Skunk's yard
and you'll get the wheelbarrow.
But hurry!"

Back in Skunk's yard,
Big Bear walked around and around.
At last the others came.
"Please," called Big Bear,
"if you will just get in line,
we can finish fast."

While they were lining up,
a small brown head
poked through the hole
in Skunk's yard.
It was Mr. Mole.
He had finished his afternoon nap
at the bottom of the well.
He wanted to get some air.
Mr. Mole was surprised to see
all his neighbors.
They didn't see him.
So he just stayed quiet
and waited to find out
what would happen.

HONE

The trading began.
Spotted Pony gave Owl
the soft pillow.
"I'm only doing this for the sake
of poor Mr. Mole,"
said Spotted Pony,
brushing his mane
with Skunk's brush.

Owl pushed the wheelbarrow
toward Squirrel.
"I wonder if Mr. Mole knows
all the trouble we've gone to,"
said Owl, hugging his pillow.

HONEY

Squirrel threw Big Bear a rope.
"Mr. Mole is very lucky
to have us for friends,"
said Squirrel,
taking the wheelbarrow.
Big Bear caught the rope.
"A rope," he shouted.
"At last a rope!"
Someone behind them coughed.
"Did you hear something?"
Squirrel asked.
"I think so," said Spotted Pony.
"It sounded like a cough,"
said Owl.

"AHEM!"

They all jumped.

There was Mr. Mole.

For a second no one moved.

Then they rushed over to Mr. Mole.

They shook his paw

and slapped his back.

"How did you get out?

How did you get out of the well?"

they kept asking.

"What do you mean?"

Mr. Mole answered.

"I just walked through my tunnel,

the same as always."

HONEY

"Oh," said Squirrel.
"Oh," said Owl
and Spotted Pony
and Skunk.
Big Bear said,
"It's nice to have you with us,
Mr. Mole. This is my fault.
When I saw you lying
at the bottom of the well,
I thought you'd fallen in."
Big Bear held up the rope.
"I was trying to rescue you."

Mr. Mole nodded. “Well,” he said,
“I can understand the rope.
But how were you going
to get me out with a jar of honey?
Or a pillow? Or a brush?
Or a wheelbarrow?”

Everyone talked at once.

"My toast was too dry," said Skunk.

"My nest was too hard," said Owl.

"My back was too itchy,"
said Spotted Pony.

"My bricks were too heavy,"
said Squirrel.

HONEY

Everyone stopped talking.
They all looked at their feet.
Finally, Squirrel cleared his throat.
"I guess we could have been
more helpful," he said.
Owl said, "We were too busy
thinking about ourselves."
"A person should never be too busy
to rescue a friend,"
said Spotted Pony.
Mr. Mole added,
"Even when the friend
doesn't need to be rescued."

Skunk had the last word.
"Everyone's invited to a party
in honor of Big Bear,"
he announced.
"Big Bear was the only one
who tried his best."
They all cheered.
"Hurrah for Big Bear!"
It was a fine party.
They had a pillow fight.
They brushed each other's backs.
They rode around
in the wheelbarrow.
And they jumped rope.

At supper
there was plenty of honey
for everyone.